ROAD TRIP

ROAD TRIP

A Novella

Lynette D'Amico

Twelve Winters Press

Sherman, Illinois

Published by Twelve Winters Press.

P. O. Box 414 • Sherman, Illinois 62684-0414 • twelvewinters.com

Road Trip was first published by Twelve Winters Press in 2015.

Cover and interior page design by TWP Design.

Cover photo courtesy the Wisconsin Historical Society, as are the photos on pages 3, 5, 17, 25, 29, 32, 43, 56, 62, 68, 70 and 73. Used by permission. All rights reserved. The photos on pages 35 and 48 are courtesy William Gabler, from *Death of the Dream*, published by Afton Press. Used by permission. All rights reserved.

Author photo copyright © 2015 Meg Taintor.

ISBN
978-0-9895151-9-1

Printed in the United States of America

Acknowledgments

Don't stop believing...

Thank you to far-flung friends and family, mentors and readers in St. Louis, Minneapolis, Chicago, and Boston, named and unnamed, including first and most steadfast readers Dianne Lee, Barrie Jean Borich, and Kira Obolensky. I'm grateful to everyone at the MFA Program for Writers at Warren Wilson College for encouragement, rigor, and example, especially Deb Allbery, Kevin McIlvoy, Antonya Nelson, Debra Spark, and David Shields. Special thanks to my generationally appropriate and inappropriate Wild Bloomers: Nancy Allen, Carla Lowe Baku, Jayne Benjulian, Allen Chamberlain, Ellen McCulloch-Lovell, Patricia Grace King, Sylvia Mann, Adrienne Perry, and Judith Whelchel. Thank you to friends Michelle Collins Anderson, Geoff Kronik, and David Haynes for accountability, baked goods, and a reason to believe. Special thanks to *HowlRound* and ArtsEmerson staff Jamie, Emma, Vijay, Kevin, and David for support and tolerance above and beyond. For their patient attention to getting this book made, I am immeasurably grateful to Ted Morrissey and Twelve Winters Press. Finally, for everything, love and gratitude to Polly.

For the Old Italians

ROAD TRIP

To begin (writing, living) we must have death.

Hélène Cixous
Three Steps on the Ladder of Writing

.

P INKIE AND I BUMPED UP TOGETHER AFTER WE had both been dumped, but my particular dumping was more like what did I expect from a shifty, Tab-sucking, ex-cheerleader who could mimic sincerity like advertising that I had the unfortunate tequila-soaked judgment to hook up with in the first place. While Pinkie's dumping was like an interminable argument about housekeeping practices—which side of the sink to wash the dishes on, the sequence of dusting and vacuuming (dust first then vacuum or vacuum first then dust?)—interrupted by infidelity, which effectively and definitively changed the subject and dirty dishes and dust be damned.

I didn't know how to escape our friendship any more than I knew how to escape my own family. Whether I liked Pinkie or not wasn't the point. She was as inevitable as the weather. She knew me when I was young and stupid. She knew the brand of cigarettes I smoked and where I got my hair cut. I knew she was afraid of laundromats and that she slept with a ratty Casper the Friendly Ghost stuffed doll she'd had from the time she was a kid.

Casper never did much to enhance Pinkie's reputation. She brought him to the only sleepover she was ever invited to in seventh grade at Linda Christiansen's. Back then Pinkie was almost skinny, with long, stringy muscles and narrow hips. She never laid out in the sun and she was never tan. She was one of those pinkish blondes with white eyebrows and red-rimmed eyes and scratchy, tiny red bumps on her calves and upper arms. Pinkie actually fell asleep. I mean who falls asleep at a slumber party? The girls put Casper in a tutu and tiara and smeared lipstick on his face. They put Band-Aids on his wrists, a noose around his neck, and hanged him from the bathroom light fixture. When Pinkie woke up and went in the bathroom, she bumped right into him and peed her pants. She told me the story like it was the Root Cause of everything that had ever happened to her from that point on. Sometimes her eyes got even more red-rimmed when she told the story. Over the years the outcome and psychological damages of the event, like the story itself, spread like a rash:

"And that's how I developed a fear of unknown bath-rooms."

"And that's why I have trust issues with women in shortie pajamas."

"And that's why I have to sleep with the bathroom light on at night."

"And that's why I have a high startle reflex and some-times dribble pee."

I thought of Pinkie as family—somebody who knew my history, who I shared history with. And like family, there were times in my history with Pinkie when our relationship became conflicted and claustrophobic, when we were greatly disappointed in one another, and slammed down the phone; when we washed our hands, walked out the door, and yelled over our shoulders *The hell with you.*

The Starks 1951

Pauline Stark died like a bird in 1951. She was one-hundred years old. She was never sick, cut, or hospitalized. She died with all her own teeth. She blew out a breath and just went away. Her great-granddaughter Myra had just been born. Pauline had outlived many of her own children. Her husband died in a farm accident when she was pregnant with her youngest. She had never been more than a hundred miles from the farm in southwestern Minnesota where her grandson Marvin and his wife Irene now farmed. Fourteen of her grandchildren went to the funeral in Buffalo Lake. Pauline

Stark thought she would bury them all.

It was Pinkie's idea. I drove my 1984 black Plymouth Turismo, the newest car I had ever owned.

We didn't leave until late in the day. We had to go shopping for snacks. We had to pack the snacks in snack containers. We had to get ice for the cooler. We had to fill the cooler with items that needed to be kept cool. We had to stop by the dry cleaners to pick up Pinkie's shirts. We had to load the car. By now it was rush hour so we might as well wait to leave until after rush hour. So we waited. We finally got on the road and then we had to stop. For dinner. Stop. We had to pick a place for dinner. We exited at Menominee but we didn't eat there. Then we exited at Eau Claire. We had to sit down in a Denny's and order a meal. And eat it. And don't forget the extra lemon with Pinkie's tea, which the waitress forgot and the tea got cold and we had to start from scratch with new hot water and new tea and another round of extra lemon.

Now it was after dinner time on the West Coast and we were just leaving Eau Claire.

The Starks 1986
Great-uncle Frederick Stark died. He played guitar and had a smooth, round face. He had three daughters who said their father didn't want to be seen in death. They wanted to respect his wishes so there was no service, no funeral luncheon. He went into the ground without words or flowers. Everyone stayed home and didn't know how to feel.

Pinkie and I first met in seventh grade at Lincoln's Tomb in the girls' bathroom. Me and Michael had come down from Minnesota on a bus. I was sneaking a smoke with Michelle Lombardo, who smelled like a cherry Popsicle and had no hair on her forearms. Pinkie came in, bounding like she did, like an oversized puppy but not as cute. More like a puppy with withered limbs and three eyes, slobbering and panting. Like a puppy that should have been drowned in the slough at birth.

Pinkie was from Springfield. Illinois is an odd mix.

There's Chicago and then there's the rest of the state: a lot of corn, toll roads, and Lincoln memorials.

Pinkie went in one of the stalls and pulled down her pants. She was whistling or humming behind the door. I got that feeling like when you're watching a contestant on a game show who just doesn't have a clue and everybody else gets it before they do and then slowly they start waking up to the fact that they are too stupid to live and you can see it happening right before your eyes on national television, right in your own living room: the collapse of an individual consciousness. Like a car crash you can't look away from. When I looked over I saw inside her elastic waist nylon shorts bunched around her ankles a pair of boy's underwear. Tighty whiteys. That's when all this started. I knew right then that because of everything we had in common we could never be friends.

We met again years later after we had both moved to St. Paul. We became couples friends, which mainly meant that in various configurations of twosomes we got fucked up together, watched porn together, gave each other rides when our cars were in the shop, and lied about our sex lives to each other. When you're licking margarita salt off each other's breasts, you don't really notice that you have nothing in common; that sober and shirted, you'd have nothing to say to each other.

I learned everything I knew about the compulsivity of attraction, the incessant whine of possibility and heartbreak from Linda Ronstadt. I spent years staring at her 1976 *Hasten Down the Wind* album cover, her bangle bracelets and bare, tan shoulders, her breasts under the sheer muslin dress. I was the shadow on horseback behind her. I was out to sea on the background ocean. I was never in the picture, and being that I was over the age of fourteen, I'd come to accept that particular disappointment. Pinkie wasn't in the picture either.

The Starks 1960

Herman Stark died, Pauline's middle boy. He was a barber and had a thin shaved mustache and beautiful black wavy hair. He became smaller and smaller before he died. His clothes flapped on his shrinking frame, his glasses slipped down his nose. When he died he was the size of a large rabbit, his enormous gentle eyes blinking behind oversized glasses. Every year on the anniversary of his death some of the old customers met at Pizza Hut and ordered the salad bar.

Pinkie wanted to chop wood and drive the tractor and light fires and trap bears and do man things. She wanted to drive the beat-to-hell Bronco. I kept a beat-to-hell Bronco in St. Paul to plow snow and push things, like dirt and other vehicles. The doors of the Bronco were rusted shut, but I'd broken out the back window and that worked fine for getting in and out, although it made for a drafty ride. I didn't pay up the insurance or license tabs so I wasn't about to let Pinkie take it out on the road. Pinkie had this idea of herself that because her hair was cut with electric clippers and she wore a man's watch, she was manly. In fact, Pinkie thought her pronounced manliness undermined the full range of her emotional expression. "People expect me to be as tough as I look, which means I always have to be the man and men are all alone in the world."

The four of us were sitting in one of those dingy gay bars without windows. My girlfriend got up from the table—to dance? Get another drink? Pee? On her way to wherever it was she was going, she walked behind Pinkie's girlfriend and touched her shoulder. I'm going to slow it all down here so you can see it: We all have cigarettes burning. We are sipping amaretto sours and fuzzy navels, bottle beer and shots. My girl pushes her chair back, flips her hair. She's got on tight black jeans and a shiny turquoise shirt with snap buttons. Those buttons. She was a drum majorette in high school. She walks like she's got on gold braid and white boots, lifts her feet like a colt. She comes around the table, behind Pinkie and her girl, Cincy. Trails her fingers along the back of Cincy's shoulders.

That's all. But in that moment I saw everything. I saw my girl stopping over at Pinkie and Cincy's to install a stereo in Cincy's Karmann Ghia. She's under the dashboard, stripping wires, Cincy is leaning in, holding a flashlight, mouth breathing.

Cincy's wearing stretchy bad underwear and it's over when she gives a little come squeak.

Cincy's panties were still wet when Pinkie came home from her job as a counselor for Bad Boys. Pinkie worked with the men who rape and fuck up the girls and I worked with the girls the men rape and fuck up. Bad Boys and Doormats. What happens when you put two helping professionals together is they both think they're due; they've been paying out and paying out, and now it's their turn to collect. It's a situation that can leave both parties a little short on generosity.

In the conflagration of breakups that followed—mine, Pinkie and Cincy's—Pinkie trapped me on the phone for hours, second-guessing the origins of lies and betrayals. Pinkie needed to know the *Why?* and *What does this all mean?* and *How did this happen?* and *Now what?* To get off the phone, I lied to her about the possibility of demeaning reconciliations with our exes and of better babes who'd appreciate us for our pure hearts and open, oozing wounds. For me, I knew all I needed to know that night in the bar. There's no point in going on when what's done is done.

Some time passed. The beat-to-hell Bronco became my longest relationship. There were other girls, some boys, religion and sweet fruity drinks, a 1993 Geo Metro, more lies and breakups. Once all that starts, it just keeps going for a while—sometimes forever.

The Wisconsin Dells is a resort area distinguished by gorges along the Wisconsin River formed by aggressive glaciers. The fog comes out after dark from the river or the gorges or the peaty boggy ghosty land. It's not a fluffy fun fog, billows and pillows shape-shifting like balloon animals: a poodle, a teddy bear, a puffy giraffe. This is hard-edged fog, dense as water; a fog that can corrode asphalt and lead a car hurtling seventy miles per hour right over a cliff into the river.

"I wore a pink tuxedo shirt with pearl studs and matching cufflinks, pearl gray pin-striped pants and a morning coat, you know the kind with the tails? I had shiny black patent leather shoes and a mustache." Pinkie relishes in her description of herself as a dude. She takes a drag from my cigarette and tongues the smoke. I hate it when she does that. We're in the black Plymouth Turismo. I'm driving. When Pinkie smiles, I can see her perfect tiny white teeth glowing in the dashboard light. Those little teeth make people trust her, which comes in handy in her profession. In the rearview mirror I can see Casper on the cooler in the back. He looks all perky and big-headed. We are talking sex—real, imagined, pretend. It's late and we need to stay awake. Casper receives all the lies we tell each other as true as the white hot flames of love.

"Gebby was dressed as Nancy Reagan," Pinkie says defensively.

I keep my eyes on the road. If Gebby were ever dressed as Nancy Reagan it would be Nancy Reagan as a size gigantisaurus instead of a size two. That's the trouble with talking sex with Pinkie—it just wasn't to my taste.

"We're on the dance floor. Marvin Gaye," Pinkie says.

Pinkie was a white girl from Springfield, Illinois, with limited self-regulating abilities. She'd shake it out after a few drinks but her dance face could cut a wide swath around her. Pinkie's story continues. There was a six-shooter, a wild rodeo ride, a snappy uplifting mustachio.

"She was a bitch on wheels." Pinkie sighs and shakes her head. "Just my type. You know why we broke up?"

Of course I know. Do you know how many times I've heard this story?

"Dish washing. G-D dish washing. I'm standing there at her sink. I'm washing her dishes—"

The Starks 1984
Nearly a dozen guinea hens died. This was the sum-

mer when the noisy flock of guinea hens were picked off one by one by raccoons because the stupid hens insisted in roosting in trees night after night. Marvin put the dogs out at night. The killings continued. Then one night he sat up on the roof of the pole barn with a shotgun. He watched three raccoons move with surprising purpose and velocity toward the few remaining roosting guineas. He shot the lead raccoon and tied the dead body high up in a tree. Then he went to bed. Later that night, the raccoons came back and ate the heads of the few remaining guinea hens. Marvin found their decapitated bodies under the tree in the morning.

"—her stinkin' crusty dishes. I couldn't stand going over there. Dirty dishes everywhere. Girl would rather eat over the sink from an open jar with her bare hands than wash a G-D dish. Said she'd rather pack up and leave town than wash a dish. So I washed them. To be nice. Which is what I am. And I never said she was a disgusting pig. Which is what she was. I might have made an indirect reference to her disgustingness. I might have gagged a little standing at her sink. I may have mentioned her white trash roots, her obvious lack of orthodontic treatment as a child, her propensity for coffee stains and unwashed bed linens. But I wasn't mean. I wasn't trying to hurt her feelings. I'm standing at her sink. I'm washing her dishes. She says I'm not doing it right. Not washing right. Wash on the left, rinse on the right. I said to her what in God's great G-D glory do you know about washing dishes? I have a theory. See a person's style of washing dishes is like a personality indicator like the Myers-Briggs. You can't be but one or the other. I washed on the right, rinsed on the left. It was a natural fact of my personality. I couldn't change my dishwashing habits any more than I could change my natural inclination for single-malt scotch and bitches on wheels."

It was a natural fact of Pinkie's personality that she had no internal process. All of her thoughts came out of her mouth. And I mean *all* her thoughts—not just what she did last weekend or what she was doing this weekend, or what her favorite dessert was as a kid, or her plan for peace in the Middle East—but everything. What she was doing right now, what she was *going* to do—making tea, taking a shower, *going* to make tea, *going* to take a shower, turning left, getting sleepy, feeling hungry, cooking dinner, eating breakfast, doing the dishes, the likelihood of the room air conditioner lasting another summer.

We've just passed the exit for Black River Falls. It'd be a different thing if Pinkie was just one of those people who talked too much. She rattled and chattered, clattered and babbled, and she wanted eye contact the whole while. She wanted you to get in there with her about what she was saying, even when she wasn't saying anything.

When she was going anywhere, even just to 7-Eleven for a Sunday paper, she had to call me and lay out her itinerary and then say good-bye a good twelve or twenty times, as though we'd never see each again, as though she were leaving on a jet plane and the soundtrack was breaking our hearts. And on her way to 7-Eleven or anywhere else, she had to have a fresh brewed cup of Earl Grey tea in the car with her, snacks for the road—peanut butter crackers, raw, unsalted almonds, and craisins, each in their individual ziplock bag—a coat or extra sweater in case it got cold, a rain jacket *and* an umbrella, and Casper, her most constant companion.

If I had any of that extra lemon from dinner I might take a big bite to wake up my face. I crack the window. "My feelings don't cozy up to me like they might with more girly girls," Pinkie is saying now, repeating another subject. "I need to dig deep and push hard. Spread myself wide open. It's not part of my masculine nature to tell you how I feel especially if I'm feeling vulnerable or insecure," she says telling me how she feels. Pinkie's gritty exterior, as she has explained to me many times, was a facade—a surface disguise—for the tenderheart she protected within. "Only my buddy here knows all," and she sets Casper on her lap and gives him a little pat. "See? Casper is a ghost and ghosts are supposed to be scary, but when you get to know him, Casper isn't scary at all. He's a *friendly* ghost, a misunderstood ghost with a sweet boo."

"Aren't you, little buddy?" Pinkie pats Casper again, who is looking all puffed up and pleased with himself.

I hate to be the one to tell her that she sounds like a girly girl flat-backed with her panties in her pocket. Why doesn't she just grow out her hair and find a big-headed bald guy to throw her down? I can feel Casper looking at me, smiling his smug little grin. Go for it, buddy.

The Starks 1986

Buddy Stark died. He was the father of Myra's first cousin, JoJo. He lived on a dry-docked houseboat on the Mississippi. The police came looking and found his body after he didn't show up for three days at the bus company where he worked driving senior citizens to the conservatory at Como Park and the Chanhassen Dinner Theatre. Buddy had a few ex-wives and a lot of hard feelings spread around but not much else. When JoJo heard about her father's death she threw a few tools in the trunk of the car, called a couple of friends, and they met at the river. After JoJo cut the padlock on the door, everybody climbed aboard and looked around. Plastic dishware, bags of empties, a couple of blue work shirts on wire hangers, a two-burner hot plate. The place smelled of mold and stale cigarettes, burnt coffee and dead fish. JoJo took everything. She shoved it all in a black plastic trash bag. She took a can of Folger's, a half-smoked pack of Kools, a pile of unopened mail, and a flannel-lined, navy blue windbreaker. She unscrewed a brass barometer from the wall, cut nylon ropes, and sliced a narrow foam mattress with a box cutter. She had the idea that everything that had ever gone missing from her childhood was stashed away on that houseboat and this was her one chance to get it all back.

This is the cheese and porn stretch of Wisconsin highway. Cheese curds with that peep show? Eating cheese curds produces a pornographic sound not unlike the sound of a squeaky bed spring. Squeaka squeaka squeaka. Pinkie and I had known each other for so long—but she peed with the bathroom door open, she wore loud print Hawaiian shirts, and for a mental health professional, she missed a lot of subtle and not-so-subtle cues, like: the line forms here, no entry beyond this point, and no means no.

It was my opinion as a helping professional that people didn't change. Born that way use them up that way. If people changed—left a bad marriage, quit drinking, overcame a fear of elevators—it was never about psychology. "You're like a preacher who doesn't believe in God," Pinkie said. "Psychology is about redemption. It's about hope. We all need saving at one time or another, whether you call it psychology or angels." She psychologized Bad Boys who were in a state treatment program for kicking the shit out of wives and girlfriends or their faggoty boyfriends. She talked to the shitkickers real slow and soft, all the time showing her tiny teeth so they'd work up to trusting her. "They are some sad boys," she told me. "Real sorry for themselves."

It's so late now it's after bar closing in most bars except a few secret after-hours clubs.

I'm still driving. Pinkie is still talking. "Which one do you like: 'The Devil Had Nothing to Do With It.' Then there's a colon and a subtitle like: 'Stopping the cycle of abuse. You are your own devil.'" She pauses expectantly. "Here's another one. 'Wits Not Hits: How To Stop Going OFF When Your Buttons Are Pushed ON.'"

What are we talking about again? Oh yeah. Pinkie's idea for a series of self-help videos for Bad Boys about anger management. I was throwing in with her game plan. We had ideas for a whole line of products—workbooks, guided imagery tapes. I thought about her sitting in a circle with big-knuckled guys, guys with beards and bellies, or sharp quick guys, the kind that laugh at everything. Her talking soft and slow, but going after them, pushing like she does. Seems to me that Pinkie would be the perfect trigger for a lot of these guys, like they could practice not kicking the shit out of their wives by not kicking the shit out of her.

Until I could afford to go back to school and take up something that required no emotional investment on my part, like business, my immediate career goal was to get out of the big chair. Talking to Doormats day after day, trying to get them to lighten up, let alone trying to get them to leave their Bad Boys who were all so bad they were irresistible, was wearing on me. Sitting in the big chair didn't make me feel smarter than or like the big lap of love. All that whining was having an adverse effect on my nervous system, causing me to smoke up a car payment or two and add to my collection of beer cans. I'd come to realize that I wasn't well suited to direct service. I didn't mind helping the victimized, at least theoretically—and if they weren't big whiners. But I didn't want to be in the room with all the blood and bruises anymore.

I used to wish that I had my own chair. A chair in my mind. It was my chair. Not a fancy, insubstantial stick chair. Not a too soft, too big, cushy chair that I couldn't climb out of. Just a chair. Mine. I could go sit in my chair and be quiet.

The Starks 1968

Myra's brother Michael Stark died. Mike was supposed to be the farmer in the family until he died. In his high school graduation picture on the wall in Marvin and Irene's parlor he had bangs, like Peter from the Brady Bunch or Karen Carpenter's brother—the guy nobody ever noticed next to his skinny, singing sister. He looked cute in the photo on the wall. When Mike died, Myra took pictures of him laid out in his coffin. You've

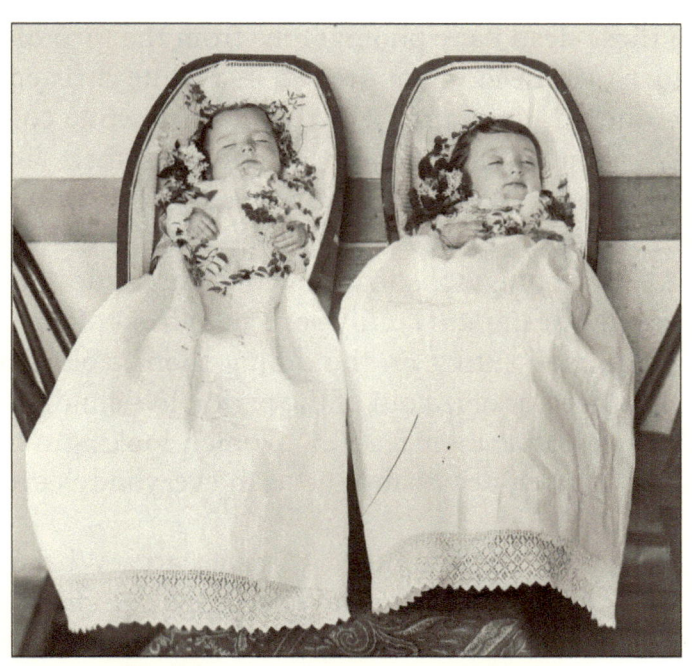

seen those dead baby photographs from the turn of the century? The dead infant dressed in a white christening gown tucked into a tiny, white satin-lined white coffin? People included these dead baby photos in their family photo albums. When company came to call, you'd sit down and open the photo album and there'd be all these dead baby photographs maybe with a curl of dead baby hair alongside the stiff family portrait in front of the new barn, the men sitting on the dining room table chairs that had been dragged out of the parlor, live children on their knees or at their feet, the women looking wrung out and somber, dead baby ghosts in everybody's eyes.

There was this one time. It was a party. Who were the party people drinking and drugging? The chem dep counselors, that's who. I had my certification. I could be the superior sober one when I needed to be. Not that night. That night I was high high high. I was sitting on a red vinyl couch. The couch made noises when I shifted or when people sat down and got up. I was wearing a wide leather belt. The belt and the couch were falling in love. Then I was a rabbit and I was sitting on a sidewalk looking at a shiny, shiny roof. It made me happy. Then I was a bird, singing my little druggy song, "One day him, the next day her. Everyday, somebody. Someday, everybody."

Party people in brightly colored dresses and skirts, in loose white pants and sandals, were dancing. Was it summer? Was this a wedding? Against the dining room wall, above the food table, slides were projected of beach scenes and sunsets, women in and out of bikinis, naked breasts with and without tan lines.

The thing I hated about ex-drunks and ex-dopers was that puffed up righteousness like now they're owed. They've made the supreme sacrifice; they've given up their one true love and dagnabbit, now they're entitled to the good stuff. They've earned it. Take Joe, who ran one of the men's groups. Joe used to drink until the trailer where he and his wife Marlene lived burned to the ground. Nobody was sure how the fire started. The insurance came through so it wasn't a total loss. But Marlene and Joe's wedding pictures were burned in the fire. Marlene said they were the last pictures of her before she put the weight on. I could tell she felt real bad about losing those pictures. Joe acted like quitting drinking transformed him into somebody good and noble, like he had saved a child from a burning building. Marlene worked double shifts in a nursing home to put him through community college to get his certification. So while Joe went off to classes and sat in Hardee's sucking down free refills on coffee studying about drinking and quitting drinking, Marlene was home alone with four kids. The oldest boy, Josh, had an invisible father who was not Joe. Josh watched the little ones and helped out some at home. He remembered when it used to be just him and his slim mom. Joe made out that feeding another man's kid was about as good and noble a thing as quitting drinking. The oldest boy was growing up round like a barrel, like his mom.

A woman fell across my lap and we were kissing. She put her soft, warm hands on my arms, the soft, wet slug of her tongue in my mouth. I pushed her away, avoiding her soft wounded eyes. There was a time when I tried to change the pattern of my attractions. I tried to be open and positive. I made a list: no debutantes, no bureaucrats, no motherless daughters. No sportos, bar trash, or depthless divas. No processing queens, recovery junkies, or stoic nonverbal primitives. No pointyheads, pinheads, or dickheads. No twelve-steppers, two-steppers, or ugly stepsisters. No unemployed, unwashed, unread, underage, underaccessorized . . . I wanted to want what I didn't want.

We went out. She called me on the phone and we made plans to meet for dinner—not a weekend dinner, not for a first date—a Wednesday. Not a small, pricey dinner-for-two place in Uptown or Mac-Groveland. Just a nice place, inoffensive food. Maybe Vietnamese. Not in my neighborhood or her neighborhood. An anonymous neighborhood. Nobody ate too much, or drank too much. Nobody stared meaningfully into anybody's eyes, or made out in the bathroom, or puked in the parking lot, or cried at the table. Success of a sort. So we tried it again with better food and a bottle of wine. Maybe we went for a walk or a bike ride, met for coffee, talked on the phone. We shared a dessert. We stopped at a bar for a nightcap. We saw everybody we knew there. We could feel that everybody thought we looked good together. We looked good together. And we should have stopped right there. That moment of getting off on everybody looking at us together. Her knee pressed against my knee, her body curved toward me. Everything opening to some future that was already happening between us. Where nothing happened. Oh, it was sex of a sort. The sort that sober grownups have in the sweaty dark where the respective parts of the parties in question are mutually, respectfully partyful. It just wasn't my sort of sex.

I had to get off this red vinyl couch. The couch was fucked up. Already my belt and the couch were breaking up. A hundred miles away I saw a little tan oasis—a gap between a waistband and an untucked shirt. That looked like a nice quiet party. I wanted to be at that party.

Some things were happening. Shiny things. With waistbands and belt buckles and rabbits with staring glass eyes. The music got really loud for a while.

What happens is sometimes I get stuck on the line. That's how I tell it to myself. You know how a comic book has text and pictures in boxes and the boxes are made out of lines? That's what it's like. I'm in one box with one set of words and images and then I jump to the next box—different pictures, different text—but it's the same story. When I land on a line, I'm not in one box or the other. I'm stuck until I get unstuck. When I was a kid I didn't think it was any big deal—it was scary exciting—like making yourself faint by bending over and panting and then standing up fast while squeezing yourself around the middle. When I'm stuck on the line, I'm looking for the way to the next image, the picture that will show me what happens next, what to say in the logical and correct sequence of events. On the line everything is a little floaty. I don't see my way to what happens next and then I'm in the next box and something has happened. But often it's a surprise exactly what that something is.

My brother Mike clued me in that nobody else was hanging out on any lines. One time when I was a kid I got up in the night and opened all the cow stalls. I can remember the sweet sharp smell of hay and manure, the warm grassy breath of the cows. The safe and humid darkness was an ancient and familiar thing. A farm is crowded with ghosts, the ghosts of animals and machines, generations of Starks; ghosts of growing things, dead things. I remember the heavy animal shapes shifting in the darkness, then the darkness becoming more dense and solid, the cows merging with the dark, the dark coming in and going out. It was hot. I felt hot. Feverish. I threw off my pajamas and I felt the dark like a blanket wrapped around me, fingers brushing my throat, a dark bird on my shoulder, a wall pushing against my back, a thick sucking mud at my feet. I felt like something more than myself, like myself inside-out. It was a feeling I could taste in my mouth, a feeling I chewed and swallowed, gulping it down like I'd never get enough.

In the morning I didn't remember getting up in the night, opening doors. I remembered the cows, the dark, the inside-out feeling. I thought it was a dream. When Dad and Mike went out for milking, the cows were all over the barn and they had to round them back up. Mike found my pajamas in the straw but he never told.

Another time after morning milking, coming in to get the little kids up for school, Mike saw my bedroom door open, the bed empty. He looked in the tool shed and my bike was gone. I don't know how he knew to look. He started walking down the driveway toward the tar road. He said he could see my bike lying in the gravel. He found me in the culvert, curled up like a possum, a caulking gun next to me. I had white caulk smeared all over my arms and legs and on every finger. I had a vague recollection of being in a box in my bed then getting caught up on a line, wanting to seal the gaps in my hands to make flippers. I remembered swimming in the air with my flipper hands, skimming and soaring through the night like a nighthawk. Then falling and falling, over and over.

That's all I remembered.

Mike rounded me up and I told him about the boxes, about getting stuck on the lines. He helped me to figure it out—and he told me to keep my face shut. Sometimes I'd get a headache and, like I said, sometimes the floaty feeling could be a little scary, but mostly I liked it. I liked the surprise of coming back to myself, of thinking back to whatever had happened, whatever I'd experienced, coming to me in flashes like a scene caught in the corner of your eye as you drive past a lighted window in a house on a dark road. You are already past, and the image forms in front of you.

Now as a mental health professional I know the whole DSM deal—blackouts, fugue states, bullshit. I'm not interested. Diagnosis is all a crapshoot. I get a bad headache from time to time. So what? Meds made you fat or stupid, or fat *and* stupid.

Sometimes it's like watching an end-of-the-world movie. When the world is attacked by zombies or aliens or giant earthworms or a disfiguring disease? There's always a clear set of choices the characters need to make to survive: don't open the door, leave the cat, pull the trigger now, run like a motherfucker. On the line, sometimes I have a sense of a faded diagram, a smeared image that indicates the next thing to do. But in my movie the world ends.

"You can thank me for saving your sorry ass."

Pinkie?

"I just stopped by on my way home and what do I see? You pouring gasoline on your career with a lit match in your hand. You could lose your license just for being there. And what were you doing with that kid from group?"

The anger and outrage coming off Pinkie could melt glaciers. I lit a cigarette.

"She wasn't my client, Pink. Nothing happened."

"Nothing happened! G-damn you! How can you say nothing? I saw you! Here."

She handed me my belt.

Why was it that Pinkie put so much damn effort into proving me a lying liar? Didn't she have other stuff to do? Why couldn't I just be messed up and stupid like the rest of the world? What did she want from me?

Pinkie was always going to be just one thing. She was always going to prefer tea to coffee, well-done roast beef to rare, sports movies where the underdog overcomes poverty or dyslexia or one leg being shorter than the other to kick the winning field goal in overtime. She didn't like to watch sports. She liked to watch movies about sports. How could anybody be just one thing all the time? I sound like one of the Doormats. "Just because he kicked the shit out of me twenty-seven times before doesn't mean he'll kick the shit out of me again." As a matter of fact, yes it does. Born that way, use them up that way.

Pinkie had a one-track version of the truth that didn't leave room for mitigating circumstances or dueling opinions. Her inelastic viewpoints made her tiresome and unpopular. It made her vulnerable and likely to get her feelings hurt, which always came as a big surprise to her. As her friend, it made me feel bad for her, but more often I was embarrassed and pissed. There are rules for life, and following the rules is what keeps you alive, what gets you through. Don't pick up hitchhikers. Wash your hands. Don't fuck your friend's girlfriend. Don't tuck your shirt in if your ass is wider than a Buick. How hard is it to follow the rules? If you don't know— whether you're faking not knowing or you're just dumb- fuck stupid—you don't have a chance. I didn't want to be responsible for saving Pinkie. Being too close to her was likely to infect me.

The Starks 1891

Farm kids grow up tough, that's for damn sure. You can tell by their missing limbs and teeth, their constellations of scars, and the ghosts of the invisible dead among them.

The winter of 1891 calves froze stiff in their stanchions. The hens stopped laying. That winter Benjamin Stark died. His mother, Pauline Stark, cooked on a wood-burning stove. When there was no fuel, she burned corn cobs or twists of straw. Pauline was a stoic, humorless woman. On birthdays, the ten or more kids got a handshake and a pair of socks for the boys, an embroidered hanky for the girls. When they married, boy or girl, they got a new Bible to bring to their new homes. There was no birthday cake, no Christmas tree, no Christmas presents. Pauline didn't want her kids growing up soft.

January 12 started out as an unseasonably fine day, snow on the ground going sloppy wet. As soon as they were out of sight of the homeplace, kids pulled their heavy winter coats over their heads walking to school. Pauline took advantage of the mild weather to wash a load of winter woolens and hang them out to dry on the wire line strung through the branches of the black walnut tree and a chokecherry.

Right after lunch the bone pale sky seemed to drop closer to the ground. The air tightened and bristled. There was a sound like a far-off train. With the roaring wind came a fine, dry dust of snow. A snow you could sweep with a broom, but that hit with the force of a shotgun blast. People trapped outside in the blizzard suffocated before they froze to death. The powder-fine driving snow made it impossible to breathe. Temperatures fell from shirt-sleeve weather to killer cold in just a few hours. Hogs wallowing in thawed mud in the morning froze stiff in the flash-frozen ground that afternoon. Schoolgirls trying to make their way home were tripped and hobbled by the wind wrapping their skirts around their legs. When the storm hit, Pauline was gathering the damp laundry. The baby, Benjamin, played in the wash tub near her feet. He was an easy baby, happy gnawing on a cold biscuit. The doctor couldn't get through because of the storm but snow must have got in his lungs before Pauline could grab him up and get back inside.

The storm continued through the week. They wrapped the baby in a flour sack and oil cloth and kept him out in the barn while the bigger boys built a coffin and waited for a thaw to dig a grave. Pauline stayed home and washed the kitchen floor the day Benjamin was buried. Come spring they found the laundry rotting under snowbanks.

Some years ago, before Pinkie went out to Colorado for grad school, she took two weeks and drove out West in her Toyota truck with the topper on back. She called her trip the Home on the Range Tour. She packed Casper and ziplock bags of craisins and almonds and lactose intolerance drugs. She asked if I'd be her contact person—the person the authorities would contact if her dried bones were found in the Arizona desert or her truck rolled off a cliff in Colorado or Mexican bandits kidnapped her and held her for ransom. I had a bad feeling, but it was like being asked to be the maid of honor for somebody's wedding. I didn't know how I could get out of it.

Every day while Pinkie was on the road, I got a souvenir in the mail from her Home on the Range Tour: a bag of sand from the Moab desert, a chunk of petrified wood from Arizona, rocks from various roadside rest stops, pinecones from Yosemite. I felt overwhelmed and burdened with the detritus of Pinkie's road trip. I didn't want the weight and substance of these mementos, but I couldn't discard them either. Like a wrong message on the answering machine, a stranger's voice trusting details of time and place to a wrong number: *I hope to hear from you. I'm sorry I didn't call. Pick me up in the parking lot at nine.* I couldn't delete these misplaced messages either. Somebody might need this information, someone might care—it just wasn't me.

There's something in me that is provoked by Pinkie. Something small and mean. Why does she make things so hard for herself? Why doesn't she get it? Why am I so hard on her when all she wants is for me to like her?

I think there are limits to intimacy—or there should be. I knew so much about Pinkie it limited any deep feelings I might have had for her. Pinkie told me that she once walked in on her parents having sex. It was very civilized. I imagined her father saying, *Thank you, dear,* her mother changing into a fresh nightgown after. I hated that I had this vivid scene from Pinkie's private life in my head. I knew she had soft hands and sensitive skin. She'd been using the same brand of yellow hand lotion since junior high. She'd had the same smell since junior high. It was a smell most people would get tired of smelling pretty quick. She hated getting rained on. She didn't like her clothes or shoes getting dirty. She wore her pants with a hard crease and had her shirts laundered with light starch. She was allergic to everything.

The Starks 1957

It was happy times then when the kids were young. Being out on that farm after she and Marvin married she never felt alone though she came to it from town and was glad to come away. Father was a stonecutter—gravestones. He lived in the big city—Minneapolis—and she and the little kids lived with Ma in Winthrop. That's just how it was then. He was a man like a wall, stone dust on his clothes, in his hair, stone in the hollow of his chest. His hands were bricks, his face like a boulder. He left his mark all over the city.

To this day, the face of Liberty marks where her father sat night after night at a tavern in the city. She never saw it, but she heard it told he slammed a silver dollar so hard on the walnut bar it was like Liberty's face was carved into the polished wood. He bent silver dollars between his thumb and forefinger for drinks. He bent them all between his fingers. She didn't drink growing up like she did. She saw how drink chiseled away at a man, a drop at a time, wearing him away.

This was the time it was Caroline's birthday. She was eight or nine and the cousins all got together then for birthdays and such. When they were all together, the aunts and uncles and all them kids, it was a crowd, you better believe it.

They were going over to Helen's right after church for the doings. They had to stop home after church so she could pick up the pineapple upside-down bars and Marvin had to check a sow that was due to farrow any minute. They only had them hogs a short while. It got to be too much with the milk herd and all, and she told Marvin she wasn't any hired hand. She had her egg money and her garden and flowers—wouldn't catch her slopping a hog. Michael and Myra were out in the yard. Myra's no more than five or six then. She told them kids to stay clean. They were just going to stop and then they were going again. They were at the old pump in the yard. The pump handle went around, you cranked it around, but if you didn't set the catch, that handle would spin back and kick you like a cow.

Michael got to messing, turning the pump handle, and then Myra wants a try. He slips the catch, thinking to be funny and that little girl turns the handle and lets go and the handle comes right around and whacks her right in the head. Whack! And she's just standing there, blinking. Doesn't make a sound.

A head is mostly bone and not bird bones either. Bone like a stone. She never was a child to cry and fuss; she was good that way. Irene pinched her sometimes just to see her blink. She never let out a peep—she'd just blink like surprise.

So they load up the car and start off. Them kids is in the back and they're not even down the driveway and Michael's crying, "Myra's bleeding. Myra's bleeding." She turns around and there's blood on Myra's face and she asks, "Where'd that blood come from?" It's from that pump handle cracked her scalp. She gave her one of the baby's diapers and tells her to clean herself up, she can't be visiting with blood on her head and she's got her church dress on besides.

All the kids is playing outside, but Myra is tight to the women in the kitchen and her mother tells her go outside and play. She says she has a headache, and what does she expect when a pump handle knocks her noggin. Darlene Breederhorst is there with the new baby—it was Danny, he joined up to the service after high school—made a career of it. Myra wants to hold the baby. So she's got Danny and they're fussing in the kitchen to get dinner on the table, and then one of the women screams, "There's blood on the baby!" And everybody's thinking the baby's hurt, so's they rush over to where Myra's got Danny and she's bleeding on that little baby! Her head started bleeding again and she got blood on the baby and all over her church dress, and you know, blood don't warsh out.

"Remember when we showed up at my parents that one time?" Pinkie asks me. I remember. We stopped in Springfield. Pinkie was picking up a new car. Her mom was a killer bridge player and did all the wheeling and dealing and car buying in the family. Living in Lincoln Land impacted Pinkie. "It was like living under the eye of God, an Old Testament God in a top hat and a rusty black suit. In the capital of the state of Illinois, the county seat of Sangamon County, the home of Honest Abe alive and dead, Lincoln was the daddy of us all. Being raised Catholic and growing up in Lincoln Land was a double whammy. My every thought, action, and intention were measured by the Catholic Church and the legacy of Lincoln. Would Lincoln chew the host? Would Lincoln fart in confirmation class and lay the blame on Bobby McVie? Would Lincoln wear his brother's underwear and pee standing up behind the bleachers?"

"Remember how your mom tried to get us to eat those leftovers? What were they left over from? Your high school graduation?"

"She doesn't like to waste food, and she doesn't like to eat, which means somebody else has to."

"I was born a statistician in a family of clinicians. It's the age-old conflict between empirical data and theory. I don't remember ever seeing my parents fight. I'm sure they did but they didn't do it in front of us kids. Conflict behind closed doors is such a setup for secrets. When I got out in the world, I had no models how to deal with conflict. Actually, for a long time I thought conflict was an indication that the other person just didn't have all the necessary data to reach the same conclusion as me. What's so funny about that? Sometimes if you consider all the options, Thai food *is* the right choice. It's a simple process that requires diligent investigation, analysis, and testing of hypotheses. A choice is an opportunity to explore multiple options! So much is at stake, whether it's what's for dinner, what color to paint the kitchen, or— what do you mean I can't call you after eleven o'clock at night? I thought we were having a conversation? Setting limits on when I can call is about you controlling our relationship. It's you setting the terms and conditions. It's you in the driver's seat. Sometimes I just want to talk to you, what's so hard about that?"

. . .

"I was never one of those girls who sexualized horses."

"Were you more into geese? Badgers?" I think I'm pretty funny.

"No." Pinkie doesn't think I'm funny at all. "I mean I wasn't all *National Velvet*, I never wanted a big pumping stallion between my legs. What about you? Did you have your own horse growing up? Did you have to do chores all the time? What did you do for fun?" Pinkie wants to know everything. She's driving for a change. Tomah is ahead, The Gateway to Cranberry County. It ordinarily might make me a little twitchy that Pinkie is behind the wheel, but the road is empty at this time of night. Pinkie has never been a member of the Slower Traffic Keep Right set. The left lane is her birthright. You'll know her when she comes up behind you, flashing her brights and honking. Just give it up and move over. Pinkie believes that if she communicates her intention, her express desires, she'll get what she wants: an open left lane, my deep feelings for her.

One day, out of the blue Pinkie started calling me by a nickname. It was cute and girlish and had nothing to do with me. I asked her why she was calling me that name. She said I needed a nickname so now I had one. I said that's not how people get nicknames. You can't just give me a nickname. Besides I don't like that name. She didn't care. She kept on calling me by my new nickname—in front of our friends, at the bar, at work. I told her don't call me that anymore. She acted all hurt. Finally she said, okay, I won't call you by your nickname in public. It will just be my name for you. I said if you ever say that name in my hearing again, I will rip your tongue out and shove it down your throat and watch you choke to death.

"We trapped barn swallows, shoved them head first up the cows' assholes. The birds flapped their wings like windmills. Bets were taken if they'd suffocate before they were shit out. That was pretty fun." I go on: "I had a horse. Ginger. She died of the swells, that's when a horse's belly bloats up."

"Well, that's sad. Did you have a funeral?"

"We hauled her to the boneyard, Benjamin's Grove. I don't know what all was buried out there. Benjamin was a baby when he died. Lots of kids died back then."

The Starks 1984

She grew up on a 360-acre farm in southwestern Minnesota that was in her father's family for four generations. The farm was eight miles outside of a town of seven hundred people. Myra looked at the same view outside her bedroom window all her growing-up years.

Her parents lived in the original farmhouse bought from the railroad in 1889 by Myra's great-grandfather, Herman Stark. Herman drowned in the corn bin, leaving his wife Pauline and the eight boys with the farm. There were one or two girls too. The house didn't have electricity or indoor plumbing until after WWII. Myra took a bath once a week on Saturday nights, in a hand-filled tin washtub. There was a shower, but a shower wasted water. The same water was used to bathe three kids, and she and her brothers fought about who would be first in the tub.

Myra's father, Marvin, was a slow-speaking ponderous German bear of a man. He wore a sweat-stained seed cap indoors and out. When he lifted his cap to scratch his bald scalp his high, pale forehead seemed to extend over the top of his head. Shaggy, gray curls fell over his collar. When he spoke Myra's mind drifted, her head turned to dust, her eyes rolled back in her skull. When he spoke Myra sank into thick water, submerged by the sound of his voice, the rhythm of his words. She lost consciousness, forgot to breathe. His speech was measured and deliberate, like he sat and walked and drove. His hands were as big as dinner plates. He smoked cheap, smelly Dutch Masters cigars and owned a fleet of Harley-Davidson motorcycles. "Fifty years of marriage, sixty years of Harleys" said the poster at Marvin and Irene's 50th wedding anniversary, studded with pictures of Marvin and every motorcycle he had ever owned, from the 1939 Indian to his 1994 Harley Classic. "Wish I'd held on to that Indian," he said. "Be worth a pocket of change now."

Marvin was tough as a boot. Years past, a steer kicked him in the back, right between the shoulder blades. "Kicked me so hard—that steer kicked me right into the next county." He drew back his arm and punched that steer between the eyes, dropped it to its knees, then walked back to the barn and finished milking. "Hell," he said, "I was walking better than that damn steer, for goddamn sure."

A farmer owned the land, owned animals, machines, had a wife, children. He worked the land, animals, machines, people. Everybody worked. Everything served a purpose. Everything served the farmer's purpose. The barn was reroofed before new shoes were bought, or new linoleum was laid in the kitchen. Machines and animals, crops and weather, were more important, came before people.

It was a farmer who in 1816 killed the first elephant brought to America. The elephant was transported at night so people couldn't get a free look. You had to pay to see the only elephant in America. The farmer shot the elephant because he thought it was a sin to charge people to look at an animal.

The new house was a cheaply made pre-fabricated, three-bedroom ranch. Myra never lived in the new house. The old farmhouse was pushed to one side and the new house dropped into place thirty years ago. Marvin didn't want to pay for the old house to be demolished, and he wanted the new house to be in the exact same spot as the old house so he could maintain the same view up the driveway. He also didn't want to see the old farmhouse torn down. "Let it die a natural death," he decreed, and so for thirty years the old house had been falling apart, naturally, board by board, bit by bit, disintegrating to a shadow. Myra's younger set of siblings used the old house as their playhouse, breaking out windows, drawing on the walls, lighting fires in the upstairs bedrooms.

When Myra visited her family she sometimes visited the old house too. The steps to the second story were rotted away, so she climbed upstairs on the risers. She opened cupboard drawers and peeked into closets. Inside the tiny closet in her old bedroom, clothes still hung on hangers. A child's dress, filthy, with puffed short sleeves and three buttons down the back, a rust stain on the skirt. She stooped under the low ceiling and looked out the window at her displaced childhood view: acres of plowed fields to the horizon, a black walnut tree, a graveyard of broken-down cars, old fencing materials, a cracked bathtub. In 1871 the Minnesota legislature passed "An Act to Encourage the Planting and Growing of Timber and Shade Trees." Farmers were awarded two dollars per acre per year for planting trees. Green ash, cottonwood, and elm were trees commonly planted. Near the tar road she could just make out a narrow strip of unplowed pasture and windbreak trees on the north side of the farmstead. This was Benjamin's Grove, where Benjamin, the youngest son of Herman and Pauline Stark, was buried in an unmarked grave.

There's a bag of mint Milanos next to me in the car. These damn cookies provoked a sixty-three-mile tirade from Pinkie. "Being that we're friends and close and all, it seems to me you could demonstrate a little more consideration in regard to my health issues. I am, of course, referring to my acute sensitivity to wheat and wheat products, which you know about because I've communicated this fact to you, and you have been witness to the debilitating and profound allergic reactions I have suffered when I have mistakenly ingested wheat."

Your throat closing up tight or your heart stopping—that's an allergic reaction. Pinkie's version of an allergic reaction was more like a headache and excessive flatulence.

"You know this, and yet," she looked sadly—and longingly—at the Milanos, "you mock me and my allergic condition—right to my face. I feel excluded from your cookie gorge fest. Excluded. And my feelings are hurt. Hurt."

Any time I had something for myself—a thought, a cookie—Pinkie felt excluded.

"A person is not a stick of wood without feelings, impervious to pain and deep-seated yearnings. No, we are not!" Pinkie is clutching Casper now, shaking him for emphasis. "If you even had two thoughts about me and how it would impact me to see you with your mouth full of mint Milano cookies mile after mile, which I can't eat, which I *dasn't* eat, you could have decided to forgo your own selfish and exclusive pleasure or a better idea would have been to include a treat we could share—share. Do you even know what it means to share? To think of someone else for a change? How hard would it be to think of a little homemade special treat of oatmeal craisin cookies with spelt flour? My most favorite ever.

Which you also know."

My thoughts about cookies or anything else are my own private business. I sigh. I bet if I could see in the dark car her eyes would be even more red-rimmed than usual. *Dasn't*? Who does she think she's talking to? That pale-faced faggot Casper?

There's a fifteen-cent toll at Highway 39 at Cherry Valley, Illinois. No attendant. No change. "You must have had a lot of good eating, growing up on a farm. All that fresh produce," Pinkie said.

The Starks 1984

It was Thanksgiving at the Starks'. Dinner was served promptly at noon—no exceptions. There was no formal or informal dining room. There was a card table pushed up against the kitchen table, cushioned folding chairs, dusty from their subterranean sojourn in the basement, opened and arranged around. Irene had put the twenty-one-pound turkey in the oven before first light. The turkey was cooked in a covered black-speckled aluminum roaster until the meat was falling off the bone. There were no golden brown drumsticks to call dibs on, no bones to pick, no crispy skin, no photo opportunities with the golden brown bird on the table, no neatly carved slices of white meat for turkey sandwiches later. There was a ransacked carcass, every shred of meat pulled off the bones—the skin and bones tossed into an old ice cream bucket for the dogs and barn cats.

In another roasting pan was the mystery ham, a thick-skinned, shaped loaf of ham-like material that had been cooking almost as long as the turkey. Irene deco-

rated the ham loaf with pineapple rings. Slices of desic-
cated ham loaf were eaten between soft white buns with
ketchup.

Everybody contributed to the dinner. Myra's sister
Caroline brought seven-layer salad and pistachio instant
pudding salad made with mandarin oranges, miniature
marshmallows, and Cool Whip. Tommy, the baby in the
family and a bachelor, brought the heat-and-serve soft
buns. Myra brought the "store boughten" pies: pumpkin,
apple, and French silk.

There was no stuffing because Myra's family did not
eat stuffing. Dressing had hot dish connotations—food
products that had been transformed into some kind of
unnatural hybrid by proximity in the same dish. Even
though hot dish was a Minnesota invention, it was not
welcome on the Starks' table. The Starks believed in the
separation of bread and meat. Also on the table were
mashed potatoes in a six-quart stock pot, a stick of butter melting on top, canned cream-style peas and cream-
style corn heated to boiling, and a fruit salad made with
canned fruit cocktail and Cool Whip. Don't forget the
pickles—two kinds—bread-and-butter and sweet gher-
kins in cut-glass dishes.

Marvin filled his plate first and passed nothing. A
fresh, hot cup of black coffee had to be within his reach
after his second bite. He liked all his meat cooked to
a gray, indistinguishable, fibrous mass. He didn't eat
chicken—said he ate enough chicken growing up that
he figured he had his share for this lifetime. Turkey was
okay because it wasn't chicken—that's what Marvin said
anyway—"I won't eat chicken, but turkey's not chicken."
Couldn't argue with that.

Tommy didn't ask for anything to be passed, but if the butter didn't come his way pronto, he said, "Gimme the goddamn butter," and if the butter still didn't come his way, he knocked over his chair and slammed outside to smoke cigarettes in his shirt sleeves and kick a car. Tommy got whatever he wanted because he was the baby and the future farmer in the family.

Irene never sat—she bounced from the table to the stove, down the basement stairs to the refrigerator for more milk, more Cool Whip for the pies. Caroline's four kids ate nothing but mashed potatoes and buns with butter. The little kids were scrawny and shrill with yellowing hair and lots of scabs in various stages of healing. Even if they just came out of a bath, they looked dingy, like they should have been hung on the line to bleach in the sun.

Everybody preferred ketchup to gravy except Myra. Myra ate at her mother's table like a crew of farmhands. Her first plate started with a layer of mashed potatoes. Then she added butter to the already butter-saturated potatoes. Next came a layer of cream-style peas, cream-style corn, and gravy poured over everything. Her second plate consisted of a meat course. She ate Cool Whip salads from a cereal bowl for dessert.

"Clean your plate and it'll be a nice day tomorrow," Irene chirped at her family.

The air in the car feels too close and damp. We are creeping through the fog, bent on avoiding cliffs and the Wisconsin highway patrol. We crest a hill. Something emerges from the fog right in front of the car, right in the middle of the road. Staggering, floating, a ghost come out of the Dells ghost fog. One arm raised as though she were trying to find her way in the dark and murk. A refugee flat broke busted from a casino or washed up from one of the water parks? I swerve into the left lane, overcorrect, and fishtail back and forth across two lanes of highway. We are awake now.

The Starks 1984

Tommy was lean with skinny cowboy hips. He wore short-sleeve shirts year round, the sleeves rolled up to show the ropey muscles in his arms. He was mean as spit and would choke a dog with one hand and punch a cow between the eyes with the other. He moved stiff-legged like his knees were already on their way to going bad. Farmers, especially dairy farmers, all had bad knees from squatting to milk cows. Tommy worked the kinks out of his going-bad knees by kicking things, mostly cars and dogs. Tommy was mean because he was the son who was supposed to take over the farm. There was no way around it after the invisible son Michael died in a car accident. And there's no way around the fact that being a farmer meant a life of dog work, dirt, and debt.

When Tommy drank, he cried about Michael. Tommy drank McMaster's and Coke when he was flush, tap beer when his pockets were tight. Tommy drank like he had already lived a life of regrets. Before he turned twenty-one, Myra took him to a strip bar on Rice Street in St. Paul. They ordered up and the bartender said they didn't stock McMaster's—Seagram's, Canadian Club, Windsor, Cutty Sark—but no McMaster's. When the bartender said *Cutty Sark*, Tommy reacted like the bartender had called him a pussy. "What did you say? What are you saying? You're telling me you don't have McMaster's? What kind of bar is this? I can go to Chuck's back home any day or night and get Mac—any time, any day, any night and we don't even have a traffic light downtown. Now, seems to me in a big city bar such as this, you'd carry the whiskey a man wants to drink. I want a Mac and Coke, now that's what I want so don't give me any of your bull." Tommy was sure what he wanted, but he drank Yukon Jack that night and Myra had to tip the bartender extra.

Girls were attracted to Tommy because of his loose cowboy hips, his stiff future farmer knees, and his dead brother. There was always some girl in the bar offer-

ing to wrap him up in her arms when he started crying about his dead brother. Tommy will marry a woman
whose child was killed when her ex-husband backed his
Ford Bronco over him. After that she wouldn't ride in
or drive any kind of a Ford, not even if somebody gave
her a Ford, not even if all the vehicles in the world were
Fords. She'd walk her feet to stumps before she'd ever
step into another Ford.

I pull over to the shoulder and Pinkie and I just sit
and catch our breath in the ticking Turismo. Pinkie is
quiet for once. Wisconsin and all its wholesome dairy-
land goodness is a version that doesn't play in the middle of the night when there might be a body on the side
of the road. My hands are shaking. "Where'd she go? Did
I kill her?" I'm staring past the windshield, the fog swirls
and churns. There! It's the biggest, fattest woman I've
ever seen. As big as a Wisconsin dairy cow. As big as a
fifty-gallon oil drum. She has disheveled, long, curly red
hair that snakes and whips around her head like something alive. How did I miss smearing her all over the
road? And what is she wearing?
I roll down my window just a crack, "Lady, you don't
know how close you came to being roadkill. What are
you doing out here?"
"I've been waiting and hoping," she says. She smiles
and shakes her head. Her red hair seems to emit sparks.
She has a crazy lady smile. I know this smile. I've sat
across from this smile a few times. I've seen this smile in
my own bathroom mirror a few times—the end-of-the-
line smile, the *try me because I'd just like to slice and dice
someone today* smile, the *it's already so late, I'm already*

so drunk, so high, what the fuck smile. She's wearing a one-piece bathing suit. And flip-flops. Maybe I did hit her. She looks a little rundown. She's got a gash across her forehead, and scrapes on her shoulder and both knees. She looks like somebody who's just stepped out of a wrestling ring with an alligator.

Pinkie and I exchange a quick look. Doormat? And if she's a Doormat, where's the Bad Boy?

"I appreciate you not running me down." She's puffing hard and sweating. "I've been out here for hours, seems like. Praying for rescue. Praying for an angel to save me, praying for rescue and redemption, praying to be found! And here you are! An answer to my prayers. A godsend. It's a blacktop miracle!" She clasps her hands together, speaking with such passion and emphaticness that all her exposed flesh shivers and quivers. It's a skin quake.

"Are you okay?" Pinkie asks, which is such a stupido question. Clearly, our lady of the highway is not okay, is something the opposite of okay. "Were you in an accident?"

"Oh, sugar, my whole life has been an accident." She's all perky and chatty now. "I was at the Elephant Lodge Casino, right down the road, with the water park?" The words are gushing from her. She interrupts her wave of speech. "You nice young ladies wouldn't have a little nibble, would you? I am just faint from hunger."

Our sturdy roadside friend looks as far from faint as we are from ladies. Pinkie hands her ziplock bags of craisins and almonds.

"Oh, *mes amis*," she says delightedly munching handfuls, "now you have twice saved my life."

I offer her a Mountain Dew. "No thank you, lovey. I don't indulge in sugar soda. Any chips and dip in there? No?" She unclasps a small handbag no bigger than a change purse and pulls out a mini bar bottle of vodka. She sucks that baby down, then seems to expand, all her skin puffing up and tightening like a bullfrog in spring. She rears back and throws the empty bottle up into the air. Inside the car Pinkie and I duck. We don't hear the bottle land.

There's what looks like to be a bruise on her left shoulder, a little crusted blood around her left ear. I can feel a headache sneaking up behind my left eye. Just a tickle. "Are you safe?" I ask and think maybe she's not the one I should be worried about.

"Oh, my gefilte fishes, my little bo-peeps, my darling crumbcakes," she brays with laughter. Her voice makes my head hurt. "A bruise, a bang, a bullet to the brain. One more for the road, shall we?" Another mini vodka, another underhanded pop fly.

She hands Pinkie the empty ziplock bags and stands waiting expectantly. We're waiting too. How did I not notice that black eye? I'm inclined to put the Turismo in drive and spray gravel. "Chickens," she indicates her massive near nakedness, "you can see I'm unarmed, abandoned, and defenseless. I don't need a safe house or stitches. I need a lift—and a stack of blueberry pancakes with melty butter and real maple syrup."

"But where are you going? Is there somebody you would like us to call?" Pinkie is asking reasonable questions while she moves the front seat as far back as it will go and climbs back in behind me. Our new friend exhales and seems to deflate. She squeezes herself into the front seat. Her unruly hair is in my mouth. It tastes of hay. Not sweet, green early summer hay. Late winter hay. February or March. Tired. I'm tired. The pudgy knuckles of her left hand are battered and bruised and she's holding a pint bottle. Where did that come from? Not from her little purse. The car leans to the right. "Well, hello there!" She has Casper on one of her lap folds. They're looking at each other like long lost friends.

"There was an altercation, let's say. Not a fight. A fight implies stakes, victors and vanquished, winners, losers. This was more of a spat. Roughhouse and tumble." She sucks a bloody knuckle. "The elephant's walk is steady and slow, his trunk like a pendulum swings just so, but when there are children with peanuts around, he swings it up and he swings it—"

That braying laugh again, and a smell more prevalent than my cigarettes: wood ash, leaf mold—is this damn car even moving?

The Starks 1984

Irene didn't so much collect as she accumulated things: multiples and heaps and stacks of things. Her kitchen looked like a refugee camp. She piled things up: ceramic cardinals perched on ceramic branches; ceramic bunnies dressed in ceramic straw hats; enamel roasting pans; plastic dishware; silver-plated serving trays; a set of blue, purple, orange, and green aluminum tumblers; ice cream buckets of souring table scraps for the dogs; empty glass jars; books on dream interpretation and home remedies; stacks of *Reader's Digest* magazines; plant cuttings in jars filled with yellowing water; three-pound cans of coffee bought on sale; rolls of nickels.

Irene was always going to clean her house. She was always going to start a diet. Her face was perfectly round. The buttons on her cotton blouse gapped open across her round belly. She wore cheap cowboy boots with knee-high nylons. A gauzy pink nylon scarf flattened her frizzy home perm in January's wicked bluster. Where was her hat? Her gloves? Buttons were missing from her gray wool car coat. Irene bounced up and down the steps to the basement where the full-sized refrigerator resided. There was only room for a small countertop refrigerator in her cluttered kitchen. For milk, ice cream, butter, she ran down stairs, up and down, up and down, running full tilt, the round-bellied, round-faced farmer's wife.

In the seventies, Marvin started thinking about the day the dairy herd would be sold off, the day his knees would finally give all the way out. He didn't want to be milking forever, tied to a twice-a-day schedule that never allowed for a day off. He expanded his fields by breaking ground at the side pasture and following the feds' dictate to farmers to "Plant your fields from fence-row to fencerow." He planted right up to the edge of the driveway on both sides, sparing Benjamin's Grove. "We should be putting in soybeans not saving out land at fifteen hundred an acre for a bunch of dried bones." Irene fretted about letting land go to waste that could be earning money.

"Your mother don't know the half of what's out there under them trees. Life is simpler when you plow around the stump."

Pinkie is anxious. I can tell because she's talking in her careful, deliberate therapyspeak voice that she uses when a client is on the ledge or holding a knife at their own or someone else's neck. "We are concerned about your well-being," she intones to our passenger. "Perhaps we should take you to a hospital? Or call somebody?" Pinkie talking her therapyspeak doesn't do a damn thing to calm me down. In fact, her meant-to-reassure voice is riling up my headache. Why doesn't she just say what I know she's thinking? She never holds anything back with me. How is it even helpful to all those Bad Boys sitting around her in a circle if she doesn't say, *You can't hurt people like that*. Just say it. I close my left eye and run my hand through my hair.

Our Passenger takes another snort and giggles at some private joke between her and Casper. When she laughs, he bounces like he's waterskiing across a boat's wake. He looks a little tipsy. All this cozy familiarity doesn't sit well with Pinkie. I hear her breath hiss between her tiny teeth.

"Oh sugar tits, don't get your boxers in a bundle. I'm

right as rain." She offers Pinkie a powdered sugar dough-
nut. Where did that come from? "I have chocolate sprinkles too, if you prefer," and pulls a white, grease-stained
bag from her little purse and a bag of cheese puffs.

"I've been down this road before, buttons. It makes
me think of a story about a local ghost who they say
gives the best blow jobs in the upper Midwest."

Our Passenger's Story

Carmella, the only daughter of a widowed farmer in
Black River Falls, was so beautiful that every day men
and boys from all over the territory came sniffing around
her father's door. Her name sounded like *caramel*: soft,
chewy candy. Carmella had no discernible bones. She
was a thick syrup, fluid and seamless. Her honey-col-
ored skin never looked oily, her gold-streaked hair, never frizzy; her forearms and upper lip were smooth and
hairless. She was sleek and glowing, and there was a rosy
pulse under her skin that made the men and boys want
to warm their hands on her. She shook them out of her
pockets like loose change. She told her girlfriends, *One
day you're a kid and everybody looks past you, over your
head. And then one day it all changes and men look at
you, and only you, like they've never seen you before. I
need to get out of this cow town and move to a big city
where the street comes right up to your front door and
there are no garages to shelter bikes and virgins.*

Carmella's father took her out of school and kept her
at home but still she wasn't safe. The sexual power of her
could shatter glass and start forest fires. Men and boys
came to their farm and asked for a cup of milk, asked for
a handful of nails. Her father sent them away. They came

back and asked if they could help to milk the cow or pound a nail in a board. Her father was desperate to protect his daughter. He built a small shed on their property with no door and no windows. Before he nailed the last board in place, he put his daughter inside and said he would let her out in time for her wedding. His golden daughter wept. Her father was not a bad man, although he was certainly misguided if he thought a few boards and nails could contain all the hotness of his one and only offspring. He had made a secret tunnel under the shed to the barn. Every day he filled a flour sack with milk and bread and cheese and crawled through the tunnel to the shed, unlocked the secret trapdoor, lifted it up, and left the sack of supplies.

So his daughter was not starving but she sat in the dark shed, hungry for the striped light that shone through the boards of the shed's walls, hungry for her school friends, the dairy cows, tampons, and red licorice. Carmella grew pale and prayed every night to the saints and angels. Her prayers were little songs that she sang after the light stripes had gone away. All the men and boys from the area wondered what happened to the beautiful daughter. They came to the farmer's house and asked for a cup of milk, a handful of nails. The farmer gave them everything they asked for, as though their questions could be answered with dairy products and hardware.

Every day now the daughter saved the ration of milk and bread and cheese her father brought to her. She made a churn from a spoon and a water pitcher and made butter from the milk. She put the cheese in the light stripes until it softened and oozed. From the butter and cheese she shaped a pale dummy girl. She gave her bread buttons for nipples, she made a wig from threads from her skirt, she made her a dress from the flour sack. She sang her prayer songs at night that sometimes sounded like country western ballads.

One night a boy passing by with his cup of milk and handful of nails from the farmer heard Carmella singing. He was overcome with longing and love. He followed the voice singing about Jesus and honky-tonking and regret that led him to the shed without windows or doors in the woods.

The boy took an ax to the shed and the daughter was so appreciative of his help that she dropped to her knees—

"Oh *mes chéries*, the road is long but our time is short." I glance over and Our Passenger is licking powdered sugar from her fingers. Are those sprinkles on Casper's face? I turn back to the road but not before I see Pinkie in the backseat leaning forward breathing the dry straw dust of the stranger's crazy hair, her tongue protruding between those tiny teeth. What the hell is she doing? I swear I see her lick a tendril of the hitchhiker's coiling locks.

"There comes a time in a girl's life when she looks around and realizes, this is not the life I imagined for myself. I could have been a radio announcer. I could have been a nail technician. I could have run away from home and joined a circus."

Suddenly I am sadder than I think I've ever been ever. More sad than when Ginger died and I watched my father from my little bedroom window throw a chain around her and haul her dead body to the grove. Sad like when Michael rolled his black Barracuda on Highway 13. Not a scratch on him. No skid marks. Like he just turned toward the ditch and the car tipped up and over, landed right side up. A black car in a yellow field. The radio was playing when they found him. *Take a sad song and make it better.* Every year after he died, Irene would bake a cake on his birthday. A yellow cake with chocolate frosting, what he liked.

"So you buck up and change your ways." What is Miss Doublewide talking about? Buck up? Try *buck up* to the fourteen-year-old girl whose stepdad kills her mom and little brother, a nice quiet murder with his service revolver against a pillow, then pours her a bowl of Cheerios and sends her off to school. Cheerio! Him holding her little dog. *Don't tell*, petting the dog. So she comes home from school and hangs that dog from the shower rod to save him. *Those poor girls.* Tears are rushing out of my eyes. Pinkie reaches between the seats and picks orange cheese puffs from the hitchhiker's jutting out chest shelf.

"In spite of life's trials and tribulations, growing up in Springfield like I did, going to a state school, suffering from allergies and unrequited love, struggling with my metal cookware phobia, I buck up everyday." Pinkie's cheese puff-flavored breath is on the back of my neck. She and the hitchhiker are giggling like idiots. Why can't they both just shut the fuck up? My head is killing me.

"We all take a tumble from time to time, a header off the bridge, a wrong turn. Sometimes it takes something bigger to change our lives, change how we live, what we believe."

That smell again. Bringing in the hay. Yellow dust.

"One day him, the next day her. Everyday, somebody. Someday, everybody."

Irene meant well, but no matter how many box mixes she tried, that cake tasted like shit.

I think there should be limits to intimacy. I never went after everything Pinkie told me. I didn't poke and pry, asking question after question. She just piled it on. She told me that before the last bitter end between her and Cincy, they decided to try to recover their dead-as-a-doornail relationship by creating a "safe place" between them. A figurative and literal place where fighting about money or housekeeping or infidelity was not allowed. So they redecorated their bedroom.

They bought a new mattress to symbolize their new beginning. A mattress untainted by the history of other lovers. They bought department store sheets and pillows and a down comforter. They spent both their tax refunds. When I was over there one time, Pinkie took me in the bedroom to show off. "The mattress has extra support, and feel the sheets. Like butter. Down pillows!" Pinkie enthusiastically threw herself on the bed. "Try it!" The sheets were white with little pale blue half-moons on them. The white pillowcases were embroidered. The bed looked pure and new, like a sailboat, like a bed in a beach house.

I patted the bed. Like butter. The bed was pretty all right, but I just knew looking at it that all that had been going on in that bed was a lot of tossing and turning, It was a virgin bed. Safe just didn't make for sexy sometimes.

The Starks 1984

Marvin and Irene roared up the driveway on the Harley Classic, decked out in bright yellow rain gear—leggings, ponchos, and hoods—looking like Danger! Danger! Like it might be a raid. As soon as the bike stopped moving, Irene struggled to swing her leg over the back of the bike. She looked up and saw Myra at the window upstairs in the old house. She waved. "I want a picture before we go on."

But before anybody had a chance to say anything more, she had something to say, "I tell him not to smoke when I'm on the bike. I tell him and tell him and he smokes anyway and all those ashes blow right in my face, *right* in my face. And I don't like that!" She stamped her foot on the ground.

"Is that what you been yammering about in my ear

the past forty miles? Couldn't hear a word you was saying." Marvin sat impassive astride the bike, a dead cigar in his mouth. The bike was small and insubstantial under his bulk. He laughed in his silent German way. "Madder'n a wet hen. Big yella hen."

"Oh, fiddlesticks, you." Irene was done being mad. She was happy to be home, happy to be off the back of the bike. "You look like a yellow chicken yourself, mister." She bounced on her toes. "I like yellow. It's a pep-me-up color, wouldn't you say?"

Marvin held his wife's arm as he stiffly dismounted from the bike. Myra positioned her parents in their yellow chicken pep-me-up rain gear beside the sighing motorcycle. Marvin tried to hold himself as upright as possible. The weight of his belly pulled him forward and his stiff farmer knees pulled him down. He didn't bounce. Irene's round face peeked out from the rain hood. They were the biggest, brightest yellow in the landscape. They were bigger and brighter than Myra's yellow Chevy truck, more yellow than a hay bale, bigger than a dead elephant.

The last time we stop, I stretch out on the warm hood of the Turismo for a minute and Pinkie joins me. "I like to look at the stars," Pinkie says looking at the stars. "Me too," I say.

Our Passenger's Story Continued
—and sucked him off like a newborn calf. Then she lit out for Chicago. The boy went back home and for the rest of his life measured every subsequent blow job he ever received against the daughter's knob-bobber job in

the woods.

When her daddy lifted up the trapdoor the next day, he saw the butter and cheese doll curled up in the blankets in the daughter's place. The little shed smelled of dairy and sex. The father felt sad. In spite of his best efforts to protect his beautiful daughter she had churned the butter just like any other girl. He would miss her looking down the rain barrel, sliding down the cellar door.

He heard a little muffled giggle. The butter and cheese doll was lying on her back, bread button eyes staring straight up at the shed roof. Wasn't she facing the wall when he first entered the shed?

Nobody knows if the daughter ever made it to Chicago. They say you can still hear her singing oh-lonesome-me songs in these parts at night. They also say you can get a few squat thrusts with her in the cucumber patch if you catch her before dawn.

I was driving a red 1996 Honda Accord. It was a bright day. The roads were dry and clear. I was driving to work, heading west on 38th Street toward Hiawatha. It was July. I was wearing my seatbelt, Brandywine lipstick, prescription sunglasses. A pale ribbon of cloth from an embroidered hanky was tied to the rearview mirror. I was looking ahead, looking forward—to work, the job I went to every day, then coming home from my job, dinner, something—scrambled eggs, leftover eggroll salad, a cheese sandwich.

I was driving to work. Pinkie and I had been out of touch for a few years. Maybe a few more than a few years. The list of rules had grown longer. I drove the speed limit. No drinking and driving. I used sunscreen. Doormats were still getting the shit kicked out of them by Bad Boys, but I didn't sit in the big chair anymore. It was July. Warm, not yet too hot. Eighties, low eighties. I ran the air conditioning in the Honda. I passed the dry cleaners, Burger King, the Somali coffee shop where slim men in shiny suits poured endless streams of white sugar into their coffee, stirring, stirring.

A big, black Cadillac Escalade ran a red light and t-boned me across four lanes into oncoming traffic. Never saw it coming. Didn't have a chance to duck or jump ship or swerve out of the way. The glass shattered in every window.

Pinkie pulled ziplock bags of almonds and craisins from her backpack and Casper. Casper didn't often come out in public. It was a sensitive subject, like praying or faking it. One of those behind-closed-door subjects. Usually, I might ride Pinkie right into the ground about making our little party a threesome, but it was almost dark out. It was a beautiful summer night. On the anniversary of our nation's independence, I'd drink domestic beer. Pinkie had a wine cooler. Tonight was July 4th and we were waiting for the fireworks.

We were at Harriet Island for Booms and Tunes, fireworks synchronized to music broadcast over a sound system and picked up and played on spectator radios. We had a blanket and a cooler. I'd been on call earlier and now here we were, our blanket spread on a little sandy dune facing the water where the fireworks would explode. I could smell the river, slow and green. July green was a promise kept. There was always a time in the dark of winter when you think, I can't go on, this is impossible. February usually. Driving home in the dark, snow-blind—the snow on the road, the snow blowing past the windshield. The promise of July.

Pinkie loved fireworks. She loved everything about them—the surprise, the color, the sound. I mean it's not exactly hard to love fireworks, but Pinkie really loved them.

I had a call today. A woman heard teeth gnawing through her roof, in her walls. Chewing. She complained to the landlord, slept with the light on, the TV blaring. She said she would lie awake in bed listening, open mouths right over her head. She knew they were getting closer and closer. She pounded on the ceiling, woke up her neighbors, blew a whistle, played Beethoven's Fifth Symphony, with the boom boom boom hour after hour. Boom boom BOOM! Night after night. Her neighbors called the police. She was cited for disturbing the peace. The cops told her to relax, to stay at a friend's house or a hotel for a few days. She was sure everybody just thought she was crazy. By this time she hadn't slept in a week, maybe longer. She went back to bed. She could hear their feet skittering right over her head, their snuffling breath.

"I met someone," Pinkie told me. She looked shy and more pink than usual. "She's a psychiatric nurse at Fairview. She used to be married. We went out to lunch. On the way back to the office it started to sprinkle. She held my arm."

I drained my beer can.

"We talked about work. She's from Michigan. We're going to get tickets for *Phantom of the Opera*. I think it might be a date."

I almost said something and then I didn't. She could have this. The fireworks were starting. A slow buildup of spraying color bouquets.

Don't stop believing . . .

Pinkie waved her small expressive hands in the air, conducting the display, singing along. People on blankets around us looked over. Pinkie sang like we were in the car in the middle of the night, windows wide open. Everybody oohed and ahhed.

The woman on the phone said she imagined their open mouths, teeth gnawing. She thought a few more bites and she'd look up to see their eyes glowing in the darkness above her. Right above her head.

Bursts of gold and blue stars rose and shivered white and silver as they fell. Blue and green tails streaked across the sky, flaming balls of light exploded into cascading streaks of color. The sky vibrated, clouds of low smoke rose from the water and floated toward shore. I reached for another beer. In the next booming illumination, I saw Casper lying back on the blanket staring straight up at the sky. He looked a little flattened. I slipped my empty beer can under his head.

That'll be the day when I die

Buddy Holly, but it was Linda Ronstadt's version.

I felt fireworks erupting in my heart. I sang too.

We were building to the finale.

She couldn't take it, she told me on the phone. She hadn't slept. She had to get some sleep. She turned the TV off, the music. She grabbed a screwdriver from the kitchen drawer and poked a small hole in the sloped ceiling above her bed. It was quiet now but she knew they'd be back. Then she put a firecracker in the hole. Just one. She had stopped at a roadside stand in Wisconsin on the way home from work and picked up a package of Black Cats. She just had to drive across the river.

She lit the fuse.

The music blasted, the fireworks boomed, the sky erupted, and Pinkie and I sang along and conducted trails in the air with our fingers. It was a spectacular show.

How could she know the wallboard would catch fire? That flames would spit and spread? She just wanted to scare whatever was chewing up her sleep, scare them away. She didn't know it would all burn.

The Starks 1984

Irene looked at her daughter across the kitchen table. They were both disappointed by what they saw. They both had coffee, lightened with milk. "Your father don't know what all I know. I know what I know. I know all about it. That woman had all manner of guns on the place. She kept them in the barn for the most part. Them days a farm wife had to do what all. Me and Marvin come out here and there's no electric power. She didn't want no wires on her land. Anybody come up that driveway she'd meet them with a gun and folks trusted she'd shoot. She shot rats in the barn, or stray dogs, foxes, raccoons, downed livestock. Whatever needed shooting. She'd sling the dead bodies into the grove. Livestock went to the renderer. Let nature take its course. Those boys of hers sat in the ditches and shot gophers for bounty. Cut off their front paws and saved them up in a sack. They was like their own country out here. Their own laws. Their own way of doing things.

"Pauline was a dreamer, like you. Not a good way to be if you're a farmer, or a farmer's wife. The only way to be in this life is to make do and be grateful if there's no fire in the barn, if the dairy herd don't dry up, wheat prices don't bottom out. That and the flowers—if I can keep Marvin from spraying too close to the house. My hollyhocks was blooming up a storm and he came by with the sprayer and they just keeled over. Dreams is going to disappoint you every time.

"Pauline, she never learned to leave well enough alone. She was always scheming about something. Don't know if Great-G even liked her much. He never said, then he up and died and left her with all them boys. She had troubles, every woman does, but I never heard tell of it. You can expect with all them kids that more than a few died. That's just how it was. There was another baby died before Benjamin, then the other'un had sugar—I can't remember which. Them boys was good to her, they grew up like a pack, never gave her no trouble, but she had her plans.

"She heard tell of a trick elephant might be for sale up toward the Cities. She got in her head that an elephant would make her rich. Change her life, change life for her boys, maybe get a few of them off this farm. Folks in these parts would pay to see something like a big elephant, like a regular three-ring circus.

"Foolishness plain and simple.

"She puts up Benjamin's Grove what was just the top forty acres then—doesn't tell the boys, and makes a deal for that elephant. Sends a handful of the boys to go pick it up. They was on the road for weeks and during spring planting too. That woman had her own mind.

"They had that elephant just a short while. Nobody figured on all a full-grown elephant could eat. Stripped the bark off the windbreak trees, ate ditch grass down to dirt, then went after the winter hay. Walked right through every fence they put around her, the cows just follow her down the road. And how you going to hide an elephant? Nobody was going to pay fifteen cents to see an animal that was just right out there bigger than life in the pasture. By harvest everybody in the county had been by for a look-see. Then the winter came on."

"I thought I might see you at the funeral." Not what I want to hear first thing on a Monday morning. "I was out of town," I say reflexively, moving to the pick-up line.

Who died? Ex-client? A colleague's parent?

"The line is here," a woman in black Lycra corrects me.

"You were close at one time, weren't you?" He sees my face. "Maybe not."

Maybe Pinkie did love fireworks, like she loved single-malt scotch and Buffy the Vampire Slayer and oatmeal craisin cookies made with spelt flour. Who knows? One thing I do know for sure, we never sat on a blanket by the river and watched fireworks and sang along to classic American rock songs. Don't you know me at all by now?

Another Story

"They also say you can get a few squat thrusts with her in the cucumber patch if you catch her before dawn."

That's one thing they say. Then there's a whole other story.

Like even the most beautiful girls, Carmella thought her butt was too big, her waist too thick, her breasts too small, her lashes too short. She could achieve the most tolerance for her body only when she was tan. A dark, seamless tan somehow elevated her physical self. She practiced tanning like a religious devotion. Her goal was to achieve a tan early in the spring and to maintain it through homecoming in the fall. She pulled her hair back with a headband and barrettes to achieve maximum exposure to her face. She smeared herself with baby oil, rotating in her adjustable lawn chair and following the light like a sunflower. She longed for spring break in Florida. The head must be tilted back, the neck stretched to eliminate creases under the chin. Fifteen minutes out of every hour she raised her arms to scorch the pale underside of her shapely limbs. Even if a beach or swimming pool had been available to her, she did not tan in any public capacity. Tanning was a private ritual, to be indulged under the relentless sun without witnesses, without makeup, without relief of any purpose or distraction except perhaps a radio, a tall glass of ice tea or lemonade watered down by melting ice. After tanning, sun drugged, sweaty, and coated in oil, she showered and lathered herself with replenishing moisturizers or soaked in a bath filled with cool water and scented oil. Tan, she was transformed, as though a great purpose had been accomplished.

One day in the city in early summer as the daughter tanned in her lawn chair, the straps of her white bikini top tied behind her back, her smooth skin glistening with oil, she saw a white girl in a fluffy blue robe under a parasol carrying a lawn chair. The white girl got set up near the daughter and spread out her magazines and sunblock and juice boxes. She was the whitest white girl under the sun, creamy pale skin like vanilla pudding. There was something familiar about her milky eyes, her white cottony hair. Then Carmella recognized the butter and cheese doll from the little shed in the woods. It was her own handmade girl. What was she doing here? She was supposed to stay on that farm and cook and clean for her father, muck out the barn and feed the chickens, hoe the cabbages and snap the beans.

The butter and cheese doll lay back on her lawn chair, opened her robe, and exposed her white white skim milk skin to the judgmental sun.

That Butterhead girl is going to melt in this sun, har-rumphed Carmella. *She's going to spread and ooze and make a mess of herself, and make a mess of everything.* The doll sat up then and smiled at Carmella. All her teeth were sharp, pointy nails. She pulled at her fingers like they were cow's teats and squirted hot milk into the hot air. The milk from her fingers sizzled and steamed. She clacked her nail teeth together and spit sparks at Carmella. In spite of the heat, Carmella felt a chill. This was the girl she had made. She was clammy and pasty, squatty and lumpy as boiled potatoes. U-g-l-y.

"Hate to break it to you, Butterhead," said Carmella, "but you're not made for life under the sun. You need to go back to the cool woods. You need to get back to the green shade of Wisconsin and lay low from public view." The Butterhead gnashed her nail teeth and wept milky tears.

Stretching her deliciously tan and shapely arms, wiping the sweat from her sweetly rounded belly, Carmella understood the lament of the poor Butterhead, a too-white fishbelly pale girl with bread button breasts. Carmella pulled off her headband and shook out her hair. The line of her neck, the arch of her eyebrow could stop traffic. The swell of her fresh breast could overturn governments.

Carmella sighed. "Hate to break it to you, Butterhead, but we girls are our bodies. We learn our first lessons about power and powerlessness, about how the world will receive us from our own faces and bodies. You need a serious makeover, my dolly." There was only one hope for poor little Butterhead.

Using her fragrant sweat and the bark of dogs, a

squirrel tail and chicken parts, Carmella gave Butter-head what she had been missing, what she needed to save her life. She put all the pieces together in Butter-head's pants and made her a man with a mustache.

Pinkie's funeral was last week. The funeral was one week ago. One week ago tomorrow. Ten days ago, Pinkie died. She was driving to work and then she was driving home and a kid coked up and drunk, driving 120 miles an hour going the wrong way into oncoming traffic hit her head-on and she died. She was driving a white 1998 Camry.

The glass shattered in every window but I wasn't cut. I walked away, shaking glass out of my hair, my shoes, like broken teeth.

There was a time Pinkie was witness to when I wanted to be a different person, fall in love, be faithful to lovers, friends, find a purpose, do good. None of that had happened. My life was the same, only the cars had changed.

A Cadillac Escalade weighs about three tons. The average weight of an Indian elephant is three to five tons.

I'm going to slow it all down here so you can see it: Mary McGreevy was driving her daughter to gymnastics. They had jelly toast for breakfast with orange juice. Jane was a little chubby and clumsy. Mary, who had been a spirit guard twirler in high school, was hopeful that practice with cartwheels and the balance beam would stretch Jane into a taller, leaner, more graceful daughter. She thought she should never have named her daughter Jane. The name itself was short and stout. *Jane.* What was she thinking? What was wrong with Isabelle? Elena? Ophelia? The boys were easier. She never thought about their bodies, their bodies now or their future bodies, except if they were clean or not. She loved her daughter. She saw a red car facing west in the eastbound lane, police routing traffic. Quickly, she asked, "What kind of cupcake will you get?" Her voice high and insistent. Startled, Jane turned her head toward her mother in time to miss the scene of emergency vehicles and flashing lights on the side of the road.

My glasses flew off my face and were later recovered in the back seat. The seat belt stopped my forward momentum into the windshield. I was hit on the passenger side. My red Honda folded in half like a closed book.

I never saw it coming.

Mike showed me the bones. We had gone out to Benjamin's Grove. If there wasn't a new carcass out there stinking up the place, we'd play funeral or army. Mike was the preacher. "O gent-lest HEART of JeSUS, have merCY on the SOUL of Thy deparTED servant. BE not severe in THY judgment but LET some drops of THY precious BLOOD fall UPon the devouring flames, and DO THOU O merciful Savior send THY angels to CONduct him to a place of reFRESHment, light AND peace. A-men."

When we played army, sometimes I was a prisoner of war and he rescued me. Or we were out on patrol. We died over and over. "They got me! Tell Ma I'm sorry (gurgle gurgle) tell her . . . It was me killed that rooster."

Mike led the patrol into a tunnel of scrappy sumacs and wild grapevines. We had to hunch and crawl. When we came out we were standing in a small clearing surrounded by aspens. I knew they were bones. I thought cow but the skull was wrong. Too big. Mike sat inside what looked like an enormous galvanized culvert pipe collapsing in on itself. A bone cage. There was a rusty hubcap impaled on a long bone stem. He turned the hubcap. "Get in. I'll drive."

Traffic was stopped all the way to the entrance ramp. The car flipped over and over. Glass and debris sprayed everywhere, like a car crash hailstorm. There was no fire—this wasn't the movies—just smoke. Thick black smoke. A trail of tire marks 124 feet long. There was no indication that the driver of the other car applied her brakes. Pinkie was pronounced dead at the scene.

The Starks

In fall the hungry ghosts emerge from hell to stretch their skinny legs. Their joints clack together like dry wood and their throats are blocked by knots. Their hunger is the relentless hunger of desires unfulfilled, of corrupt secrets and regrets. Maybe they died without family or connection. Maybe no one held their hands at death, no one washed their cooling bodies, no one sang to them. Maybe they died by drowning and lost connection with the earth. Perhaps they were murdered or they died in a place that was not their home among strangers. In hell they've only had fire or blood to eat. While we pull out our sweaters and gather our crops and caulk our windows in preparation for winter, crows take up their demanding bleating and we duck our heads and avert our eyes. They're angry and hungry and they want to be fed.

Black River Falls Journal

Authorities are looking for the woman who fled the scene after an altercation with a man at the Elephant Lodge early Sunday morning.

The woman, a guest at the Lodge, had been at the water park early in the evening and then spent several hours at the Lucky 7 Buffet.

According to witnesses at the scene, a man described as undertaker pale with a mustache approached the woman at the pie and pudding station and attacked her with a cup of milk and a handful of nails.

The man is in custody. The woman, a robust redhead, is said to have fled the scene wearing a bathing suit and carrying a banana cream pie.

"Oh saints and angels. A bruise, a bang, a bullet to the brain. The driver's door was open. She was slumped to the side, hanging out. Right on the side of the road. The police hadn't arrived yet. I went to her and called her by name."

I was driving to work, the route I always drove. Pinkie's drive did not resonate with me. I felt no impending doom, the traffic light blinked no signal for misfortune, just the usual stop, go; red, green—the clock pulsed eight-twenty. Pinkie was dead. It was a simple fact. I don't know if it was an especially terrible or sad fact. I had lost time, lost opportunities, lost the chance to share more of her company, lost our friendship. I remembered the smell of yellow lotion, Casper, her tiny white teeth. I remembered these things like a story I'd heard when I was young and stupid. It was a long time ago.

The glass shattered in every window.

I'm ready to be done with this road trip. I leave her to her life.

The Starks 1891

The storm came on so quick, Pauline didn't remember the elephant at first. The boys got the dairy herd out in the morning and the elephant just went along. Once she wanted to do something, or go somewhere, it was more trouble than it was worth to get her to change her mind. She was probably hungry too. She was always hungry. After fall harvest the boys had taken to feeding her acorns and silage to try and fill her up. Sometimes the silage was fermented, and she'd get tipsy and pull the roof off the chicken house, scatter the woodpile, crow back at the rooster.

There was no real meanness in her but hunger made her bear down, pull out fence posts, knock the cows away from a hay stack, she put her head and shoulders in the milk room, just reach out with her long trunk and suck up gallons of fresh milk.

She had turned out a disappointment as an investment but she was a pet of the county. Neighbors came by with a treat for her—split watermelons, a sack of sugar beets, young willow shoots. Dogs liked her fine. Pigs too, though she made the horses a little skittish. The boys slung a rope saddle on her, and then climbed up, had a basket weave chair seat up top. Like going for a ride in a high-wire hammock, an elevated rocking chair lurching through corn and wheat fields to the slough, the dogs threading under and around her tree-trunk legs. She was the highest point on the flat horizon. It was always a shock when Pauline would look up from the yard and see her out there—a vision of another world on the prairie.

One of the girls ran out to open the barn door for the cows that were scattered out in the pasture. The straight-line winds nearly trapped her in the yard. She was crouched by the south wall, sure to freeze. The yellow dog found her and she grabbed his collar and they crawled back to the house together. Pauline lit the lamps and put water on to heat. She was walking the floor, clutching Benjamin, calling for her boys. The bigger boys had linked arms and waded home. They couldn't walk through the deep snow on the road so they followed the fence line. They passed what appeared to be a big snow pile until they got right on top and realized it was two horses huddled together, covered in snow and ice, sunk to their bellies. The boys had frozen toes and ears, frozen fingers, but they all got home safe.

In the morning they shoveled a path to the barn and started counting their losses. Snow had piled up in the elephant's empty pen. Benjamin was starting to cough.

All of her thoughts came out of her mouth.

The beat-to-hell Bronco pushed the bones along the asphalt. The bones of dead babies and horses, dead motorcycles and barn swallows, teeth and dirty dishes, tighty whiteys, a pillow with gunpowder burns, empty beer cans, tequila bottles, and Cool Whip containers, the empty chair, elephant bones, a 1984 Plymouth Turismo, a Toyota truck, a black Barracuda, a Cadillac Escalade, a white Camry, a stuffed doll.

"End of the line," I said to Pinkie. "I'm so glad we had this time together, but hasta la vista, baby. Vámanos. Arrivederci. Let's pack it up and move it out."
Pinkie flushed like a girl and wailed. She blamed me

for my coldcold heart, which was just fine with me. "We all have our own ghosts," I told Pinkie. "We're all alone in our own heads, our own hearts."

Dead as she was, it took Pinkie months and months—maybe even years—to get out of Dodge, to have her feelings about the pain of fated love, the bitterness of friendship betrayed, the cars undriven, the roads closed to her.

The day she finally left and got on her own road, Pinkie handed me Casper. He was in a two-quart size ziplock bag. His once ghostly white exterior was discolored and gray and there were bald spots where the plush had rubbed off like he had mange. He looked like he'd been exhumed from a grave. He looked like some of his friendliness might be worn a little thin. His wide plastic button eyes looked at me with reproach and dismay. He knew I'd never love him. "I want you to keep Casper for me," Pinkie said, her voice choking with something like sensitive ghost emotion. I was already feeling haunted.

When Pinkie finally drove away in her Toyota truck after standing too close to me, smelling like yellow lotion while she said good-bye for the twelfth or twentieth time, with her ziplock bags of raw almonds and craisins, her travel mug of Earl Grey, I was a little filled up with all her feelings. I was so filled up with *her* feelings that I couldn't see my way clear to what to do next.

I climbed in the busted-out back window of the beat-to-hell Bronco. I had a tow chain with a big steel hook on the end. I wrapped one end of the chain around the tow bar of the Bronco and then impaled Casper on the hook. I hooked him right through the neck. He looked at me like he expected it. Then we went for a ride.

I drove up and down the highways across Minnesota,

Wisconsin, Illinois, Casper dragging behind the Bronco through the dirty snow and sun-bleached asphalt. I
drove through the crowding and chatter, the smell of
gasoline and exhaust stronger than the smell of Earl
Grey tea and yellow lotion. Every time I turned around
and saw Casper bouncing behind the Bronco, I shook
off more of Pinkie's feelings and felt my own feelings re-
turning. It was a long drive. I drove up and down the
highways, grinding gears, crossing lines, careening off
the snow walls on either side of the road, tires spinning,
steam pouring from the radiator, no brakes.

About the Author

Lynette D'Amico worked in publishing and advertising for a decade. Today, she is a former ad writer and a graduate of the MFA Program for Writers at Warren Wilson College. Her work has appeared in *The Gettysburg Review*, *The Ocean State Review* and at *Brevity* and *Slag Glass City*. *Road Trip* was a finalist for the Paris Literary Prize and, as part of a collection, for the 2012 Flannery O'Connor Award for Short Fiction. She is the content editor for the online performance journal *HowlRound*. Born in Buffalo, New York, she has lived in St. Louis, Minneapolis, and Chicago. She makes her home in Boston with her love Polly Carl, but she has a prairie eye.

Photo by Meg Taintor

The book is set in Adobe Minion Pro. Minion is a digital typeface designed by Robert Slimbach for Adobe Systems in 1990, and Minion Pro was added to the family of typefaces in 2000. Minion was inspired by Renaissance-era type.

www.ingramcontent.com/pod-product-compliance
Lightning Source LLC
Chambersburg PA
CBHW021934170626
46807CB00007B/3096